AF427775

Aedre the Slut Wife 1
Copyright (C) 2022
By ACTJ

Copyright © 2022 ACTJ

All rights reserved. This book or any part thereof may not be reproduced or used in any manner whatsoever without the express written permission of the publisher except for the use of brief quotations in a book review. Any references to historical events, real people, or real places are used fictitiously. Names, characters, and places are products of the author's imagination.

First printing, 2022.

ISBN: 9798422179220
Imprint: Independently published

Author Notes and Warnings: All characters in this story are 18 years and older, this is a work of fiction and as such do not try this on your own.

Wish to Support me

If you wish to support me and my work, please visit the following sites for updates and for deals.

https://www.patreon.com/actjerotica

https://subscribestar.adult/taion-books

http://www.actj.ctkdjane1.com/

Hotwife Aedre

My name is Aedre, and my husband asked me this weird question one night if I wanted to maybe have someone other than him to have sex with. At first, I told him no, and why would I as I felt the two of us were happy together. I started to wonder if he was starting to have an affair or wanted to have one and as such if I was ok to have sex with other men then it would be ok for him to sleep with other women.

So, I then said as I asked him point blank, "So are you wanting to have other women to have sex with as well, is this why you asked me this question?"

He smiled as he replied, "No Aedre I asked this, because I wish to share you with another man."

Taken back from the question and the new idea of him allowing me to be shared with another man, I then asked as I wanted to make sure my ears were correct in what I heard. I asked, "Let me get this straight you want me to have sex with another man, correct?"

"Well yes if you want to, and by the way I am not wanting to have sex with another woman, I just want to make love to you." He answered me as he then added, "Look I am sorry but a thought came to my mind that I would be having sex with you as another man just put his seed inside of you, thinking of how that will feel as my penis slide in and out of you as it is lubed with another man's cum, for some reason or another is making me horny for some reason."

When he said this, in a lot of way I am getting a bit horny as well, as he my husband is wanting to share me as well as to allow another man to have sex with me. I sighed as I wondered would this be such a great idea with so many other things going on that we should allow me to have another man to use? I closed my eyes as I sighed as I listen to my husband and what he wanted to say about this idea.

I then thought of another man that I wanted to have sex with that would be someone I would be ok seeing naked as well as seeing me naked as well. I then saw the man that I wanted in my head, and I knew who I wanted to be shared with, however I don't want some stranger in our life, I want someone who is my lover and is wanting not only to have sex with me but also loves me as well.

I opened my eyes, and I said, "I know who I want to have sex with me, however I need to know something first."

"Ok what is it that you need to know?" He asked, without asking who the other man is.

I then answered him, "I want to know what will happen if the other man gets me pregnant?"

"Well, that is what turns me on, knowing that the other man maybe the father of our child, think about this for a moment." He said, as he went on, "The both of us are young we have a lot to live for and a lot of things to hold dear, yes I love you and I also wish to have a child with you as well, however won't it be our secret knowing that our child is your lovers child?"

I sighed as the idea of the man whom I want to have sex with is the father of a child that does not even exist yet. I then smiled as I looked at him as I asked, "Will I be label a slut if I agree with this, if someone finds out?"

"As far as the two of us know, it will be our secret and the lovers." He said, as he went on more, "So as long as the three of us do not say anything we should be fine."

I let out a sigh of relief as I then told him who I wanted, and he smiled as he seemed to know that I wanted him. The two of us then talked more about things as he said he will get in contact with the man I wanted to have sex with, he then said to me that what will happen is a get to know meeting, if sex happens then I will be alone with him as he and I have sex in our bedroom. However, at some point he wants to have a threesome, in which both men have sex with me.

Agreeing to this idea, I then told him that I am fine with this, and to let him know I am open to receive his penis in any hole that I allowed him to have sex with me. So, in short I am open to have oral, and anal with him as well, the other thing is my husband also talked about maybe having him stay with us longer which I am not against if this works out, that way if I am indeed pregnant when I do get pregnant that he can be there for me as well.

So, he will make the call like I said, but it is getting late and the two of us do need to rest for the next day. So, in the morning he will be giving him a call and get things setup for the three of us. I also have a feeling that he also has some other things planned as well but I won't know till this whole event happens, I am in a lot of ways both excited and scared at the same time, as I am not sure what this will bring to our lives as we move through the years together.

As the two of us head to bed, I then decided that I want to make love to my husband at least to both thank him for allowing me to be shared and to also reinforce the bond the two of us have. As he has not yet came to the bedroom yet, I turned the light on as I entered the bedroom, I then closed the door, as I started to strip off my clothes, I would have keep my under garments still on, and wear some Pj's but not this time. I am not doing this to award my husband for allowing me to be shared but as a way to say thank you as well as to give him one last time of me not being a shared wife.

I then head over to the bathroom that we have in the bedroom, there I took one of the towels that we have hanging in there. I then went back to the bed as I laid back down as I had the towel with me. Laying there waiting for my husband to come into the room, and to see that I am waiting for him, I am sure he will be very happy to see that his wife is waiting for him so that the two of us can make love.

Although, I don't want the sharing thing to be where the one I am being shared with just comes and then leaves me. I want someone who will love me as well as my body as well. Because in short, I want to make love and not be fucked, I want whomever I am with to touch my body and feel me as he slides his penis in and out of me.

Then what I was waiting for came as the door opened up and my husband came in as he did, so he saw that I am naked and waiting for him. He smiled as he asked, "So is this an award for me to allow you to be shared or is this something else?"

"It's not an award dear, it is my way of saying thank you, as well as my way of saying please make love to me, before I am shared." I answered.

He then shut the door, as he then started to get naked, I stayed on the bed watching him undress. After he got to his briefs, I then saw that he is already large and wanting to fuck me. I grin as I laughed, as I did so the last of his clothes came off, as he made his way over to me.

He then asked, "Want me to eat you out or want to have 69?"

"I want 69 I want you to use my mouth as you eat me out." I said, with a smile.

He smiled as he then climbs onto the bed as he then started to lick my belly button as he made his way on top of me as his cock was now at my mouth, I then took his large thick member in my mouth as he is now using his tongue to pleasure my every inch of my vagina. As he did so he started to thrust in and out of my mouth, I did not mind in fact I liked it as he is using my mouth.

As he got my pussy more and more wet and ready for him to fuck me, I was getting his cock larger and ready to lay siege to my vagina. After a bit he got off of me as he then moved my legs on top of him as he did that, I lean forward giving him clear aim at my pussy and ass. So, he had a choice of plowing either hole if he wanted to.

I then felt as he placed his penis head at the opening of my anus and I gasp as he is going to take my ass with no lube, I then asked, "Are you going to take my ass, even though I don't have any lube in me?"

"Do you want your ass done or your pussy?" He asked me.

I grin as I said, "I want you to do me where you want to do me at, even if my ass is not lubed."

I then felt as he put his head in my pussy instead and he said, "Don't worry next time your ass rather lube or not will get some love too."

I grin as I know he will indeed do that and I never said he couldn't go inside my ass, even without lube. I do love anal, even without lube I am one of those who are lucky that it doesn't hurt much and the more a man does me there the better it feels. But right now, my pussy is being plowed and with each stroke he goes inside of me, the more I moan.

As I moan, I said, "Fuck me! Take my pussy use it I want you to do me and to love me."

As I say more sexual talk, the more he pounds me, and the more he touches me as he does so, he starts to come closer with his lips, soon he will own my mouth as he does my pussy. As his lips then touch my lips he puts his whole tongue inside of me, as I close my eyes as I rock back and forth. Moaning even with my mouth being used with his tongue, I can still moan.

He is not fucking me but making love to me, as he knows how to turn me on more, and to make me feel good. Yes, I do like to be taken and to be made to be the bottom so to speak, I want my men on top of me, as the make love to me. Not that I won't go on top of one, but the fact is if I am on top then who is really fucking who. As such if I wanted to fuck, I will be on top of him and not me on the bottom, taking it and being the one below. I know I am a person, but in bed I am my husband's wife and as such I like to be taken.

Then the moment I was waiting for he started to pound me deeper and faster as he keeps kissing me, he is about to fill my pussy with his sweet cum. Which knowing this started to make me orgasm, as I did so it made him fuck me harder and deeper. As he wants to go in me as deep as he can so he may be able to not only take my pussy but to get me pregnant with his child.

He then spewed his seed deep in me as he stopped thrusting as he stayed still as I felt his penis pumping in me, as the two of us still are locked both in our mouths as well as our sexes. He then slowly sided out of me, I could tell he is still very large, and he stopped kissing me, as I looked at him wondering what is next.

As he took out his penis from my pussy, he then moved the already hard head to my ass, I grin as I realizes he is about to take my ass as well. He slowly entered my ass, as he did my body started to get used to him, inch by inch. Now it does hurt mind you, and I won't ask anyone who is not like me to be fucked without lube but for me, I can put up with it.

Slowly he went as deep inside of me as he can, as he went back to my mouth as the two of us started to kiss again, I shut my eyes as now it is my ass's turn at the love. I put my legs around him as he stayed there for a bit, as my body got used to him inside of me. Then he started to pound my ass like it is my pussy.

As he did so I was already used to him and now it feels good, as he fucks me in my ass. This time at sex is more for him then for me, but he is still making love to me. What I mean is there is no way my bowels can give him a child, so he is fucking me to please him but at the same time he knows I like anal sex. Although I prefer lube, but he also knows I can take anal without any lube and not complain about it much.

Then like my pussy he then had to come in my bowels as well, as I rocked back and forth as he is now fucking me faster and harder, as he wants to fill me with his seed again. As he did so, he sent me into waves or orgasms as my body is trying to understand why his cock is in my ass and not in my pussy, but at the same time loving every thrust he is doing to me.

As he does so, I squeeze on his cock making him even hornier as he fucks me even harder. Then the moment of him to come in me came as he started to grunt and moan as he just stays in me as deep as he can go in my bowels spraying me with more cum. He then stopped and the two of us moved as he is still inside of me as he is too tired now to get out of me, and the two of us have each other in an embrace. It didn't take long before the two of us fell asleep even with the light still on.

I guess it is now morning when I woke up, as I did so my husband is now gone, I assume he is dress as well. He for sure wore me out, as he fucked me basically all three ways, although he did not come in my mouth. Although I am not sure if I really would want to do that after he did my butt or not, anyways I then got slowly up from the bed as I was both sore and stiff as the sex, we had last night was very intense and it did for sure felt very good.

As I got onto the floor I then head to the bathroom as I had the towel with me, I then started the shower and I wanted to get showered up as well as cleaned up. Not that I didn't enjoy the sex that my husband and I had, I just wanted to get cleaned up also from the sweat and grim from last night as we slept. As I showered, I am wondering how I did not hear my husband showered and get dress, but I guess I was so out of it, as well as tired from when we made love that I am sure I didn't hear him.

Sighing as I jumped into the shower as the water and the warmth of the water is helping to relax my body from being sore and tired from what I did last night. I then started to both clean myself as well as to relax at the same time, after a bit as I was done with the shower. I then came out of the shower and used a clean towel to dry myself off with, as I then put the towel up on the rack that I have in there.

I then took the old one that I used last night and put it into the bin where we have the dirty clothes at. As I then went out into the bedroom, I then collected my clothes I wore the other day and put them into the bin. Then I went to get clean clothes for the day, as I did so I then got dress as well.

After I was dress, I then left the bedroom, and to see where my husband is at. I then found him sitting in the dining room and having coffee and eating something. He saw me and he smiled as he said, "I didn't want to wake you, but you seemed to have slept right though everything."

I smiled back as I said, "Well yes, I guess you wore me out."

He laughed as he then took a deep sigh as he has some news to tell me, he then looked at me as he said, "Well I talked to him, and he is ok with this, but he is also wanting to do this sooner rather than later. I told him if this was ok, that you would be open to having sex with him today if that is ok."

I nodded as I said, "Yes that is fine if we do this today."

He then asked, "Now you do remember that it will be just you and him, I will not be in the room as you two do your thing?"

"I am aware of that, so long as I feel safe and being in our bedroom will make me feel safe anyways." I answered him.

He nodded as he then said, "Well he will be here in about four hours if that is not a good time, I can change it."

"Nah that is fine, I was going to ask if this was going to happen today or another day anyways." I said with a smirk, as in truth I want him to pound me like my husband did last night.

My husband then noticed that I took a shower as he then asked me, "So were you expecting this to happened today, as I see you already showered already?"

"Well, I woke up sweaty and since we went to sleep after we made love, I figured it would be a good idea to wash up." I answered, as I then added, "I wasn't sure if we would be doing anything or not today."

He then smiled as he said, "Its fine, I was just teasing you, as you know how we like to tease one another."

I smiled as I nodded, which is very true the two of us like to tease one another. We do it as a way to show that we love each other and that we can each take each other's personality. However, the truth is this, in a couple of hours another man will join our family and I will have two lovers one being my husband and the other a man that I have feelings for, but we never got married.

So, I wanted to prepare myself for him, and the fact that in the bedroom that my husband first took me after we got married that this friend will also take me to be his as well. When I said prepare myself for him, I don't mean to take a shower or to bathe I mean mentally get myself ready to the idea that I will have another man enter me. I am not afraid of the fact that this other men was at one time someone that we both had feelings, but neither one of us had sex. So, this will be something a bit awkward to say the least with the fact that a man that I almost married will be now having sex with me.

I then said to my husband, "Well since we have some time, I will get something to eat so that way my stomach can settle down as well as some coffee as well."

"Sounds good, I already started the coffee, and I would suggest something light to eat now." He said, as I went to the kitchen to get myself something to eat and some coffee.

After I got myself something for breakfast and some coffee I went to the table and started to eat as I wanted to not think about things all that much. For one thinking about it too much started to turn me on more and the want of having him have sex with me was even more so than before. I did not want to be too turned on to the point that I wanted to have sex now. I wanted to wait for him to come here so we could talk, even while we were undressing or naked that way we can talk about things.

After I ate and put up the dishes I had a couple of cups of coffee, that way I could relax some more, as it is getting closer for the time he will be here. As my nerves and body started to act up, not just in fear of the unknown but the wanting of another man to touch my naked body and to have sex with me. The other thing is this other man is someone that I considered to marry at one time, but the truth is I still have deep feelings for him still as well.

As the time draws ever closer to the time that he comes over, I started to grow more excited and less scared. As I knew him before, and to be honest I didn't hurt him, as we came to the decision not to go deeper in our friendship. I ended up marrying my husband whom I also knew for a long time as well, I think it is funny for some odd reason the reason I married my husband instead of my other friend is I just knew one day the two of them will be with me.

My husband then came over to me as I was on my last cup of coffee and said, "He will be here soon do you want to get ready?"

I was still thinking as I did hear him, I also wanted to think about things as I was sipping on the cup of coffee. I then sighed and looked up at him as I said as I asked, "I thought it will be to talk first then the sex comes afterwards?"

"I figured since you and him already know each other that the two of you could do whatever in the bedroom, while that happens, I will be inside here waiting." He said, as I could tell a bit of sadness or even a change of heart in his tone.

I then went over to him as he started to walk away from me, I put my hands on his shoulder and I asked him, "Do you not want this to happen?"

He sighed as he turned to face me and he answered me with a smile, "I do want it to happen it is just now I started to feel maybe this is not a good idea, however I know you will be with someone you knew."

I then smiled as I then said, "Well I guess I will wait for him in the bedroom then."

"Are you going to get undress or are you going to wait for him to come into the room?" My husband asked me as if he wanted to know what to tell him when he comes over.

I then answered him by saying, "I am not sure yet, I might be named for him, or we could talk in there and see where it leads too."

I then turned and headed to the bedroom, as I did, I let out a small sigh as I feel perhaps, I will be named for him so he could see me naked. As I got to the bedroom door, I then opened up the door as I did, so I entered the room. The room is only lite by the sun light that is coming though from the window, however no one from the outside would be able to see either me or anyone else in there naked or having sex.

I then shut the door, as I did so I then made the choice to undress that way he can see what I am sure he will be waiting for. The fact is the two of us already know of each other from before, but we never seen the other naked beforehand. Since my clothes are clean and that I just took a shower before I then neatly put my clothes as I got naked on a dresser that I could reach it when I am ready to get dress again.

I then went into the bathroom and took out the same towel from the bin that I used for sex last night. However, I smelled it to see how bad it stunk or not. It wasn't bad, as it can be said it smelled like someone put his cum onto it. Which is what it is to be used for, I then got onto the bed and waited for him to come inside. I laid on my back as my head facing the door waiting and ready to have sex yet once more.

As I wait my heart started to beat faster as I did the night that I gave myself over to my husband, but this time it is to a friend who could have been my husband. Growing more excited and not scared at all, I am starting to want to feel him have sex with me, even if he does me in all three holes the fact is he would have taken me like my husband has. I am more than prepared to accept his seed in all three of my holes, and I wonder if my husband told him that my anus can be done even without lube.

I started to grow even more horny thinking of him taking my ass with no lube as he plowed his cock deep inside of my ass till, he fills my bowels like my husband has done. However, I want to now focus on the here and now, and not what could happen or may happen. I want to be ready more than anything else, although he will be the 2nd man, I slept with I am not afraid. However, I wonder of something is my husband truly ready for me to do this, as what if I want more men after this.

I laughed about it as I don't think I will ever become a slut, but the fact that I am allowing myself to have sex with another man who is not my husband makes me wonder about myself as a wife. I shock it off and said to myself that this man I known just as long as my husband and he is a perfect fit and choice for me to have sex with.

After a bit the door opened up and he comes into the room. He then sees me naked as he shuts the door, he smiles as he asked, "So Aedre you are waiting for me I take it?"

"Yes I am." I smiled back as I said, "I am sorry I didn't marry you instead of my husband, but I want to correct that, I want the both of you."

He nodded as he sighed as he started to undress as he did so, I grow anxious as I want to see how larger and huge his cock is. He then said, "Your husband told me about this already and I agree as I am not seeing anyone, and I am not married."

After a bit I then saw his cock, and I gasp as I tried to show the gasp to myself and not to him. His cock is beautiful is huge larger and thicker than my husbands. I want it in me badly, I know it will hurt but I don't care about that right now, I want him to fuck me. As he came over to me, he then asked, "So what do you want to do first?"

"I want you to fuck my ass, no lube." I said, with a grin.

He then looked puzzled at me and asked me, "You want me to fuck your ass with no lube? Wouldn't that hurt you?"

"Has my husband tell you that I can take it without lube?" I answered him as I said.

He laughed as he got himself prepared and like my husband did last night lifted my legs up on him, he had easy access to either hole. He this put his head off his penis at the opening of my anus, as he slowly pushes it into me. As he did, I shut my eyes in pain and pleasure at the same time as I squirm around as his cock slowly went deeper and deeper inside of me. As he gave me what I want I opened my eyes panting as he was not even half way in me as he touch my breast and then my face and then moved my legs as he went all the way in with a powerful thrust in me as he started to pound my ass.

He then said as he started to pant, "Your ass is tight but feels very good, you seem to be taking this well."

I nodded as he then went for my mouth as the two of us started to kiss as we made love, as like before I rocked back and forth with each thrust into me and then as he slides his penis out as he did his thing in me. I put my arms around him as well as my legs as we both enjoyed the feeling of our skin next to each other as his penis plowed its way in and out of my bowels feeling everything that my anus has to offer him. As he did my ass and has his tongue in my mouth, I closed my eyes as the two of us pant and moan.

The pain from him in me was just a few seconds and as now has turned into pleasure as he is doing my ass like it is my pussy. As he is still in me, I said to myself I want him to take me in all three holes that way he can do me like he would have if the two of us were married legality but now he is making me his wife as well. I want to have both men, as my husband's but I know only one of them can be legality mine.

After a while he started to grunt and moan as he then did one powerful thrust inside of me as he stayed in me as I could feel him pumping his load into me, I sighed with relief as my ass has been calmed down in the way of being horny. He then slowly went out of me, as he did so I then removed my arms and legs as I opened up my eyes.

He rises up as I smiled at him as I said, "Thank you that felt great."

"We are not done yet you do know that." He said with a smirk.

I then smiled as I said, "Oh I know that, I want you to fuck me in all three holes."

He then got off of me and then got into position that my husband did last night in which to do 69. I though hmm we are going to have oral right after he fucked my ass. Well, I then said to myself oh well this is kind of kinky, but I am open to it. I then opened my mouth up as he got himself into position as I took hold of his cock, I saw that other than cum that was left over he is clean.

I put his cock in my mouth as he started to thrust his rod up and down in my throat. As he did so, he started to lick my pussy, we both moan as our sexes is in the hands of our mouths. As we both tasted each other as we both did oral to each other, he is doing my pussy and I am doing his cock. As the two of us did what we did to each other the larger and thicker he became in me. I closed my eyes as I messaged his balls making him more urge to not only fuck my throat but wanting to spill his seed down my throat.

The thing is what I did not expect to happen was this, we both climax at the same time. As he did the same to my mouth as he did to my but as he went with one powerful thrust as he started to spray his sperm down my throat, I then in turned started to orgasm as well. As I made sure every drop of his seed went down to my stomach, he did the same with me, as I started to release my own fluid and it is not pee.

After a bit he then relax on top of me as his cock is still in my mouth as I tasted every drop of his seed, I started to suck on his cock like that of a baby who sucks on his or her mother's breast. After a bit I got him once again large and ready to once more fuck me. He gets off of me, and then he did what he did to me before when he did my ass.

However instead of my ass that he entered he went deep into my vagina. As I gasp as he went deep right away, however my vagina is nice and lube with his spit as he well washed my pussy out with his tongue as he prepared me for this. As he went down again so the two of us could again connect again with our mouths, I moved my legs around him as he slowly and steady pounded my very wanting and waiting pussy.

As his tongue entered me, I then tasted myself in his mouth I tasted my pussy and to be honest I liked the tasted and I greedily wanted more of this. As the two of us made love with each other, although the last time he was doing me faster this time he is taking his time to make love to me.

He then pulled himself away from my mouth as I opened my eyes to ask what is going on he asked, "Do you want me to come in your pussy too?"

I smirk as I said, "Yes please come in me, if you get me pregnant then so be it, I want to have your baby."

He grins as the two of us started to kiss again, as he then started to pound me even faster as if he wants to make me pregnant with his seed. Although even if he does get me pregnant it is hard to tell as I just made love to my husband last night, so his sperm has more of a head start then his. Either way it doesn't matter either way.

After what seem like forever, he started to come in me, as the two of us moaned I then grabbed his hair as I still want the taste his mouth is giving me of what my own sex taste like. I am sure he as well tastes his own sex in my mouth as the two of us did have oral sex. As I felt his seed fill me up, I once more had another orgasm which if I didn't release an egg last night this for sure would have made me release one now.

It took a bit for the two of us to recover but even as he was coming in me, he keeps thrusting in and out of me. Then once he was done, I moved my legs and arms as he then rolled over on the other side of me on the bed. I opened my eyes and turned over as I did, I could feel his seed move with me in both holes.

I smiled as I said, "Thank you felt great."

"Same with you, however Aedre you do know I have kinks that I am sure you may not like." He said,

I then asked him, as the two of us touch each other as an after sex way, "Like what you may not be too surprise in what I like or not like?"

"I am not sure if you would like to be tied up as both me and your husband has sex with you." He said as the two of us looked at each other.

I smiled at him as I said, "I won't mind that at all."

He looked surprised as he didn't know what to say. I then gentle push him, so he was facing up, as I then went on top of him this time as I took his cock which is again getting large again. I then asked, "Do you want to play with my tits as you fuck me?"

He grins as I went on top of him as his cock went straight into me as I slide my body up and down, he then started to play with my breast and at times sucked on them as the two of us had sex once more. I will for sure pay for this as I am already sweaty, and I can feel the soreness come into play, but I want him to fuck me as many times as the two of us can.

Taking longer than it did before as I was doing all the work this time, in many ways I am the one fucking him and not him fucking me. Then after a while he sprayed once more in my pussy as I sink down on his chest as he started to hold me as he started to shake with each time, he came in me. I wanted to rest and now he can do me as many times as he liked this way.

Not sure how long we were in there, but I soon fell asleep as he was doing me, I then awoke later on still naked, sweaty and now feeling sore from the amounts of sex that I am not used to having so close together like this. He was not in there and I slowly looked up as his clothes were gone, I then got up slowly. I took my towel and wrapped it around myself like that of a diaper as I made it out of the bedroom.

I am still naked as my breast are still expose but this is after all my home, as I made it into the front room, I then saw both men were sitting in the living room. The two of them were talking about things, whatever it is they seemed happy about it. I made my way into the front room where the two of them could see me they turned to see me.

Both of them smiled as they knew I would come out naked or at least half naked. My husband asked me, "Aedre are you sore or do you want more?"

"I am fine and yes I am sore, but I could have more if you two are wanting more." I answered him.

He then smiled as he got up and said to me, "Well we were both talking and the two of us would like to do you together, however there is a small catch to this."

"So, what is the catch?" I asked wondering what it maybe.

They smiled as he said, "For you to be tied up as we both have sex with you."

"That sounds hot, but we don't have anything to use to tie me up with." I said, as I wondered about things a bit more.

He then laughed as they then brought out a bag filled with cuffs that could be tied to a bed or whatever they want to use it with. I then understood what is going on. I nodded as I said, "I am ok with this."

I then took of my towel and sat down naked on one of the chairs that is there. As the three of us talked about things, and the next adventure, as well as other things the three of us could do. One of the ideas is to share me with other men as well, just to get me used to having other men have sex with me and other things as well.

However, these events will be in the future and have not happen yet but will happen. As we also set the date for me to be tied up as the two of them use me. The idea is no anal, but both my mouth and pussy are fair game. It is set for tomorrow, which I have no issue about.

Hotwife Aedre Tied Up

Hello my name is Aedre and my husband as well as I have invited another man in our life. This other man is a man that I was going to marry at one time, but I decided to marry my husband instead, not because the two of us did not work out or anything, but life got into the way and other things happen. Well, my husband asked me if I would be ok if he shared me with another man and I said OK with it after we talked about things a bit more.

Anyways both my husband and my new lover are now here, and I just got done making love to my lover and I am in the front room of our house naked still talking to the two of them. I guess the two of them want to have a threesome with me while I am tied up, I said I am open to it. The reason I am open to it is because I do want to experience new things in my life as well as the same old of course.

The problem is with the same old things, as the same old is what we as a people are used to as new things can be scary however, I allowed myself to try something new by allowing myself to have sex with a man that I wanted to marry first and in some ways today was to make it where in short I have two husbands. One being my legal one and the other as my lover, however I have to also understand he is not legality married to me, and as such can still find someone else to marry or be with someone.

The fact is this I am fine with all of this, as now there is no turning back from my new life style. Also, the fact that I do love both of them, and to be honest I would have wanted to be married to both of them and not just one of them. As I think what I am saying now, as the three of us talk, I then had a thought. Since they want to have a threesome anyways, but with me tied up. Why not have it where I am not tied up first then when it works out well then, we can move to the next stage which is to have me tied up as I have sex.

So I then asked them as the two of them were talking as they thought I was done talking about what will happen I then said, "Why don't the three of us have a threesome out here in the living room, but where I am not tied up, that way we can say this is practice and that way we can do this right once we are in the bedroom?"

"Hmm I like that idea." My husband said, as he adds, "So you will not be tied up out here, right?"

I then answered him, "That is right I won't be tied up out here."

My other lover then added, "Well we can try it out that way we can see who this will work when you're in the bedroom, as the couch will work well for a make shift bed for now."

All three of us nodded in agreement, as we got the couch ready to be used for the bed as the two of them have sex with me here just to try the threesome out. However, they will only do my vagina and mouth for now, as the threesome where I am tied up those two holes will be the only two holes that will be used.

After a while we decided to give this a try so I got up and went on the couch as I laid down on the couch and position my legs and myself so that it would be easy for who has sex with me to have easy access to me. After I got myself ready the two of them then got undress as I was already naked from having sex before with my lover from before.

After they both got naked they then went over to me as my husband came over to my mouth as he gentle moved my mouth towards his already erect cock, as he slide it down my throat as he started to thrust in me, then my lover I could feel as he is starting to lick my pussy and to get my vagina ready for him to once again enter.

Then after a bit I could feel as his head off his penis entered me, like it did before. As he slides his whole rod into me, I gasp even with my husband's cock down my throat as I started to moan. After I caught my breathe again, I went back to having my husband's cock go down deep down my throat. That way I can enjoy his rod down my throat as my other Lover uses my vagina for his pleasure.

Knowing that this will be similar how I will be done on the bed, but instead of free I will be tied up as the action happens. As my lover has my legs on top of him as he has his chest and head high as he has sex with me, my feeling is he will come inside of me first then, my husband will go after him, whatever happens I am ready for it.

After a bit, like I thought my Lover came in me, then he went out of me then my husband took his place, as he did, he smiled as he looked at me. I turn to see my lover sit down next to us as he watched the two of us make love. As I looked at him as my husband started to put his penis into my waiting hole as he started to slide in and out of me slowly as he did so I could feel that my vagina is very well lubed from my lovers sperm that he put inside of me, which only made me more horny as he did me.

As my husband started to touch my neck and breast as I panted and moan as I smiled at my lover as he like I said watch the two of us make love. He smiled back as he started to jerk his cock once more, after a bit he got up and went over to me and I opened up my mouth as he slides his cock into my mouth. As the two of them once again were making love to me.

I closed my eyes in pure joy as the two of them used my wanting body like a slut that I have become. However, I am not anyone's slut I am their slut and theirs alone. Unless they want to both add more to the mix, now I am not against that but for now I rather just two men in my life. That way I can enjoy sex with the two men I have always loved.

As my husband is now trying to get to the point where he can come inside of me that way, he can fill me with his seed which I didn't mind one bit, as my lover is using my mouth again, he gentle rubbed my hair and touch my face as he did my mouth. I didn't mind one bit as the two of them were having fun using my body.

Then after a bit my husband started to grunt and moan as he started to spray his seed to add with my lover's seed as well. He then thrust as deep into me making sure that every drip of his seed sprays in the right location which doesn't bother me one bit. Then after a bit I started to get excited as my lover is doing my mouth in such a way that I realizes he wants to come down my throat, I didn't mind after all I gave my body to the both of them.

As I was just thinking of things the moment came as he too started to grunt and moan as he did one powerful thrust down my throat as he started to spill his sperm down my throat as I could taste his seed as it went straight down to my stomach to help nourish my body. After he was done coming in my mouth he slides out of my mouth.

Now that we have had our first threesome well at least I have had my first threesome, that I have ever had. Now I wonder what is up now, do we shower or are we going to head to the bedroom to finish the next leg of this? Well, I will have to see won't I.

My husband then said, "Ok Aedre I am going to get the things ready in the bedroom, just stay out here with him for a bit."

I then slowly got up from the couch as I nodded. As my husband took off with the rope that will be used to tie me in place, my lover and then looked at each other. I smiled as he did too, and I said with a sigh, "I am sorry I didn't marry you, I thought it would be for the best, after everything that has happened to you."

"Its fine Aedre, look we are together now." He said as he smiled as he gentle touch my leg as his hand is heading towards my sex.

I then put my hand on his hand as I helped to touch me as he reach my pussy he started to finger me a bit more, I then asked him as I said as I did some moans as he fingered my pussy, "That is true, I hope you liked having sex with me now?"

He smiled as he said as he went over to my lips as the two of us started to kiss as I reach over to start to masturbate his cock. He then stopped for a moment, and he answered me, "I do love having sex with you and I am happy the three of us can be a thing, but I have a question do you want a child?"

"Yes, I do." I answered with almost a snap.

He smiled as he said, "I was wondering because I know both your husband and I do too. But how are we going to work this, Aedre only one of us can get you pregnant."

"Its fine, I mean you will be living here with us, right?" I asked, wondering if I heard my husband right.

He laughed as he answered me, "Yes I will be living with you and your husband. It would save me a lot on rent, and I will help with some cost here around the house as well."

"Do you want to make love again, while we wait for him to get done with the bedroom?" I asked, as both of us were masturbating each other to the point that he was nice and erect, and I was wet and waiting for another go.

He sighed as he answered me, "Sure but I want to have you on all fours if that is, ok?"

I got up and I then went on all fours on the couch. I then looked at him and asked, "Is this what you want?"

He laughed as he said, "Yes."

He then got himself behind me as I sighed as I felt his hands guide his head off his penis to my wet pussy again, then I felt him like I have now a couple of times as he entered me. He then started to thrust in and out of me, as he did, I started to moan as I started to moan, I closed my eyes. I keep myself as straight and as still as I could as he is fucking me.

I then started to hear myself moan even louder as he started to go deeper than he was able to the other times he has done me, then he started to thrust faster as he said, "I am about to come in you again."

"Go ahead I am yours I don't care if you or my Husband get me pregnant." I answered which kind of surprise me since he has already come in me now a couple of times.

As he started to thrust in me faster and I started to moan louder as it felt very good, he was hitting some good spots, not that they didn't before. But damn this felt good, then I started to feel an orgasm coming, I then said, "Oh my God fuck me harder now please I am about to come now!"

He then started to pound me faster as well as harder as I asked him too, then I rolled my eyes back as I started to orgasm, as I let out a loud moan and scream of pleasure. Lucky for me I recover pretty quick. As he started to come in me, as well I just waited for him to be done after he was done, he slowly got out of me, and as he did, he then sat down next to where my legs are, however he gave me enough room to get off the couch.

As I moved myself off the couch my husband came back and he smiled at me and he asked, "Are you guys having fun?"

He nodded and I answered, "Yes of course."

"Well, the bed is ready now, so once the two of you are ready, we can do this now if you still want to be tied up as the two of us have sex with you." He said,

I nodded as my lover, and I then got up and the three of us headed to the bedroom. Once I was in the room, I saw that the bed now had an addition that being said. There are now four ropes connected to the bed, so that my legs and arms will be tied to the bed, my husband had some pillows in the middle to cushion me, for when the two of them do me my back won't be sore afterwards.

Knowing that the two of them want to make love to me once more, I then climb onto the bed, and I laid down on the pillows that were on the head of the bed. As I got myself ready my husband and lover then both started to get my arms and legs tied up, but they didn't tie me up too tight as there are cuffs that came with these ropes that they could easily get off of me if need be.

After I was firmly tied up, my husband asked me, "Hon are you feeling comfortable, well as well can be being tied up?"

"I feel ok, I don't hurt or feel any pain if that makes sense." I answered him.

He smiled as the two of them then started to get things ready, then my lover went onto the bed as he came over to me. As he headed over to my head, I knew he wanted to do my mouth and I opened up my mouth happily to receive his rod. As his rod entered my mouth and started to slide in and out of my mouth, as he started to make love again to my mouth as I am tied up.

As my lover is using my mouth to make love to me, I then felt as my husband came over and started to eat me out to taste not only me, but the many loads I have in me. Moaning as the two of them are giving me oral bliss, I only wonder for how long they will be doing this to me, as in making me feel love. Moaning as the two of them did their thing and enjoying the moment that I have with the two of them, I started to wonder how long this will last as in me being with the two of them.

After a while my husband then stop eating me out and then started to get himself into position as I felt the head of his cock enter me, as I felt him enter me, I let out a silent gasp as now I had both of them doing me. As the two of them did me as I am tied up, I am just in bliss as I am enjoying the sex that the two of them are giving me.

Then my lover started to spray his seed in my mouth as he went down as far down my throat as he could as he was coming inside of me. I then grinned as I tasted his seed, as it went down my throat into my stomach. After he spasm in my mouth for a bit as to get as much of his seed down my throat as he could he then took out his rod out of my mouth and I opened my eyes as my husband is still making love to my vagina.

I smiled as my lover then leaned over and the two of us kiss, as his tongue then went into my mouth, I once again closed my eyes as he tastes his sperm as I am sure I still have the after taste in my mouth. As we both do that, my husband then took his hands and started to gentle hold onto them as he went back and forth inside of me.

After what seemed to be a couple of hours which I knew was more or less a couple of minutes at the very least, that my husband started to come inside of me. My body, now completely sore, and been used very well, I have never been in such a state of bliss that my body then gave up as I blank out of what happened next as I was overcome by a surprise orgasm that I had no idea was about to come to me.

I woke up later, not sure how much time I was out, as I woke up the light is off, and I don't think it is night as there is still light from the sun coming into the bedroom. I am no longer tied up, I assume they let me free as soon as they were done with me and untie me so when I get up I can get up. I then sighed as I started to get up to be made aware that my body is sore and stiff.

After all I have had sex more times in a couple days then I ever have had sex before. I have had my first threesome, and also my first tied up threesome as well. As I took my legs off the bed, and I landed on the floor, I then slowly tried to get my footing as I once again started to stand with some issues staying upright as my body almost has to relearn to know how to walk.

As I got my balance back, I then started to walk around the room, as the door is closed, I figure that maybe they let me in here to sleep off of what happened. I am sure they understood that I had a massive orgasm, so I then went to open the door, as I opened up the door. I then walked around the house to find them.

Still naked, I went towards the front room to see what is going on. I knew it was not night yet, like I said I just wanted to see what is going on. I should have although put a towel or something over me, but I figure this is my home too as such I have all the right to be dress whatever way I want to be. As I made it to the front room, both my husband and my lover were sitting down on the couch watching something. They had their backs turned towards me, so I can easily walk up towards them, as the two of them I could tell they were watching something.

I then went behind them silently as to see what they were watching, at first, I thought they were watching a porno which kind of upset me when they have me here and able as well as willing to have sex with them. I then saw that the two of them were dress and watching what appeared to be the news as it was talking about some current events that is going on in the world, then it went to local news. After that the weather, as I watched with them, they still didn't know I was behind them, as they seemed glued to the TV which I didn't mind one bit.

I smiled as I saw that both of them got along together, which helped me feel that this whole thing will work well. I then decided maybe I should go ahead and head back to the bedroom, and shower. In a lot of ways, I am surprise they didn't smell me, as I could smell myself, not that I smelled bad, just sweat and come smell as to after sex will bring to you.

So, I went back to the master bedroom, there I will get ready for a shower, and get out clothes that they could easily take off of me, like an undies and a crop top undershirt that I have for sleeping. As I got my clothes ready, I also got the shower ready as well, I am not sure if I will have another session with sex with either the two of them at the same time or one on one. But I wanted to be ready for when it happens, this way I won't smell in the morning, and I will for sure need to take a shower.

I then went to take my shower as I had everything ready for tonight, although I expected to be molested as I am taking a shower. Although I shouldn't say molested as it will be by choice and not by force. Still, I smiled as I shower my body, I wonder what will be happening if and when they realize I am up as they for sure will hear the shower on, and I am sure they will know it is me.

After a while I then realizes they must really be into the TV shows that they were watching, but anyways I was done with my shower. I then got out and dried myself up and I then went into the bedroom, there I got my clothes on that I was going to wear. I then decided I am going to check up on the two of them, as I can hear some talking as well as some laughing coming from the front room.

As I then went into the front room, again but this time with my night time clothes, which I do wear when it is warm. I then saw the two of the still talking and doing man stuff as in talking about what they were watching. I then again silently went over to them, and I then waited to see if they would see me there waiting for them.

After a while as I could see my two lovers are busier and concern with watching TV as well as talking to each other, I then said, "You know I been here for a while and yet the two of you have not paid any attention to me?"

They then turned towards me, and they looked a bit like they were stunned to notice me there, then my husband said, "I am sorry Aedre, but the thing is you know how it is when we start to watch the TV and watch our shows."

I grin as I said, "Yes I know, and now I have to put up with two of you instead of one of you."

"Hey I am sorry, we thought you would be out for a while I mean you had a huge orgasm, so we figure just to let you sleep it off." My lover said,

I then answered my lover by saying this, "I understand that, however at least I would expect the two of you to at least noticed that I am here, I only agreed to this, because of two reasons, one that I will be with two of the men I have loved and the other reason, I expected to be able to have a man wanting to lay with me anytime I want."

My husband then sighed as he turned off the TV and he then stood up as my lover did as well, then my husband said, "Look Aedre I didn't know that is the reason other than the fact that you would be with the both of us. So, are you wanting to have sex again?"

I then realizes I got myself into a trap yes, I wanted attention but now I am in a bit of a pickle as now both of them now knew that I wanted them both for sex as well, as the fact that I love them. I then smiled as I answered my husband with a sigh, "I do but I am not sure if I want to be tied up again."

Both my lovers grinned at me and one of them commented by saying, "Look Aedre you wanted our attention and you wanted sex so how you get it is between the two of us men and not you."

Then my husband said, "Wait a bit, I have an idea, Aedre would you want both of us to fuck you again or one at a time?"

"Either way, I just don't want to be tied up again, well at least right now anyways." I answered him,

My husband then said, "Why don't we have it in the bedroom or do you want to have it out here again but this time we do anal and vaginal instead of oral and vaginal?"

We all agreed, then he said, "See it will be harder to have it anal if your tied up."

Then the two of them started to get naked as I went to get the towel that we were using before. As soon as I got back with the towel, they were almost completely naked, as I got there, I handed the towel to my husband as he placed it on the couch that we will be using. Since all I needed to do is take off my shirt and my undies there wasn't much for me to take off, it is also possible for someone to fuck me even while I am wearing my undies or what I have on. However, I don't wish to soil these clothes I do want to use them tonight when we all go to bed, or if we choose to all be naked that is also just as good as well.

I then started to get naked as well, as I said it won't take much effect on my part getting naked. After all, three of us were once more naked and this time we have already known what each other looks like and everything else, I felt almost like I would if I was not naked but dress. I am not ashamed of the way I look around them, and I can tell they are also not ashamed of the way they look around each other as well as myself.

My husband then went onto the bed, as I figured out what they are planning on doing. I then went over and got on all fours as I moved to get comfortable as I started to give my husband oral sex as I got my body into position so that my lover could take my pussy or ass, which ever one he chooses to do today. After I got myself ready, and I started to suck on my husband cock, I am not planning on having him come in my mouth. The plan is to get him large enough and he will be in my pussy, however if he comes in my mouth then so be it.

I know my ass or pussy will be keep busy as my lover does either one of them while I do what I am doing to my husband. After I got myself organize on the couch, my lover then positions me where he wanted me. I then felt as he got himself comfortable as I then felt his head of his cock starting to enter my rear end as I close my eyes to ready myself for his cock to fully enter me, as I said before I can take anal without lube.

Sliding his cock deep down into me, I gasp a bit, as yes it hurts but I can manage it. After a bit, I started to go back to what I was doing before as he started to pound my ass, like it is a pussy. Unlike the last time I had anal, this time I have both of them here at once as they both are having sex with me, but either way I think after this I am done for a while, I just kind of need this.

As I sucked on my husband rod and taking anal from my lover, all three of us were moaning at the same time, as we were giving each other great pleasure. As my lover spanked my ass as he fucked me, and my husband started to play with my hair as he saw my ass being taken by my lover, we both smiled at each other, as he started to thrust on his own in my mouth.

I then started to help him out as I knew he wanted to come in my mouth as he watched me be taken by my lover. I started to blush as I could feel it, as my lover is started to get ready to come in me as well. It didn't take long as the two of them, although not at the same time, started to come in me. Even so my lover keeps thrusting in and out of me, as if nothing is happening, I could tell he likes my ass, which I didn't mind at all, as in my opinion it belongs to both of them now.

After my husband finish coming in my mouth and after I swallowed every last drop of it down into my stomach, he then helped me as both my husband and lover gentle moved me on top of him. As my pussy was in range for his cock he entered my pussy, as my lover is still in my ass. Without missing a thrust in me, the two of them now made me a sandwich as my lover went on top of me as he gently kisses my back as my husband, and I started to kiss as well.

I am now at their mercy as they their cocks plow their way into me, as they make me have a state of bliss, which made me unaware of anything and everything around me. The only things my body and mind knew was two very well hung and thick members are inside of me, giving me what I wanted. I hunger for their cocks in me, and now I am getting feed.

As they did this to me, I thought maybe it wasn't a good idea to shower, and that I should have just did this instead of showering. However, it is way too late for that now, as they made love to my body, and as they did so they tell me they love me and want to make me have their children. With each trust inside of me, I didn't want anything else but to bear their children, all of them. I wanted to become a mommy, not by one of them but both of them. I wanted them to make me be pregnant, I gave myself fully to them and I will do what they want of me, however I am not their slave.

They both knew that I am not their slave, but that I want them to do what they are doing to me, and that as long as it does not hurt me, I am fine with it. One may say fucking my ass without lube is hurting me, and yes it does hurt at first, however I don't mind, that pain I can deal with. As I am allowing them to do that to me, as it feels better for me the longer, they are in my ass.

After a while, the two of them keep on with what they did bringing me ever so closer to once again having an orgasm. Then it came and it was liken to the one I had before that put me out, but this time I gasp onto myself as it came hard I wanted to stay up. I was able to keep myself from passing out, as I felt both of them come inside of me.

I opened my eyes after the two of them came in me, my lover then slowly got out of me, and as he did it felt good. He then went over to the chair next to us still out of breath and panting, as he did so he sat down. He didn't see me as I watched him, I then looked at my husband and he is now out cold. I then heard a phone rang from Abeodan's phone that is my lover's name.

He then went over to his clothes to get his phone, and as he did so I then slowly and quietly got up. As I did so I knew I was dripping cum from both ends as I walked slowly towards him as he had his back turn as he answered the phone.

He asked, "Hello this is Abeodan?"

I then could hear what sounded like a girl, I then said to myself, "My husband told me he was single and not seeing anyone, could he be with someone, and I not know it."

He then said, "Yes I know, about what your husband asked me however I am with someone I care about more, so."

I grin as I realizes that he might have had planned to do what he is doing with me with another couple I then realizes he loved me, and I went over him I put my arms around him as I put my chin on him still naked which scared him.

I whispered in his ear, "Go ahead and do it, but I want to know more, also I am Bisexual my husband doesn't know it and I would love to try it as long as you keep this a secret you may fuck whomever you want, as long as I can also have some as well."

He then turned to me and asked, "Do you want to come with me in the other room?"

I nodded as we both went into the bedroom, as he put the phone on speaker, there was a woman on the other line, and Abeodan then said, "Change of plans looks like I am free, however Aerielah since you and your husband know about this and he will not be there to see this, can I bring someone else with me?"

"Who?" She asked with a bit of a demanding tune.

I then answered, "Me."

"What you're with another woman, how dare you." She said, as I then butted in,

I said, "Yes he is with me, and he has been a good friend and almost my husband, however I offer you this, you want my lover to have sex with you then be ok with me there as well."

"Look I want his seed in me, and I don't want him fucking you instead of me." She said,

"His sperm will indeed be all yours, but I will make this deal, I am bisexual, and I don't want my husband knowing I know most women are." I said, as I went on, "So here is the deal we have sex, and he can have sex with you whatever way you like as long as your open to having sex with me too."

Silence on the other end, and then she sighed, "Your right I have always wondered what sex would be like with another woman, I maybe game as long as your healthy and do not have any diseases."

"Well, I have only been with two men, and one of them is Abeodan, if that helps any." I said, as the two of us talked.

So, after we talked the two of us started to make plans, the next day. We will do it at a hotel room that her husband paid for. One of the questions I asked would her husband joined in and if so, I told her that my husband would join in as well as long as she doesn't tell my husband I am bisexual and open to that yet. But if she wanted three men to do her or watch her husband and my husband as well as Abeodan bang me I am open to this.

All three of us like I said, planned on how to do this, and perhaps all five of us could become one family and this would be interesting as there will be two women and three men, after thinking about this it started to turn me on again. Either way this will be what I wanted, however instead of moving into the way of a Hotwife I am think I am heading into something else.

The End

Glory Hole Wife Aedre 1

Hello my name is Aedre and here I am naked and looking at a hole that is in the wall of a booth that people come and view porno videos at. My husband wanted me to try new things with others so that is why I am here, although he knows where I am at, and he knows fully well that I will have other men inside of me. He also wants me to record as it happens as he wants to see how I perform, I also suspect that he may also want to sell what I am doing online, however I am not going to question or confront him right now.

The reason is he gave me the money and what I needed to do this, and he told me that he wanted me happy and wanted to share me as he wanted to expand things between him and I. Although I am not really sure why, as we do have a decent sex life as it is, but hey I may as well make him happy, as he does allow me to spend his money as I myself do not work.

Since I am already for what will be happening to me here, as I keep an eye on the glory hole waiting for the first chance that I see and hear someone on the other side, I will check to see if they were indeed interest in me or not. I would say, giving my age, and the fact that I am a woman, more likely I will be able to find at least one guy and maybe more who will want to fuck me. Unless they are gay or something, then I shouldn't have any problem finding someone to fuck me here.

So, as I wait for the first man to come, as I watch the glory hole, I also am watching the video that is being shown in the room, I have enough cash on me, to keep it going for a while at least, this way I can be here for a couple of hours. Like I said my husband gave me all the cash I need to keep going till I feel like that I am done for the day.

I do sense that this will not be the only time that I will come here, as in for what I am doing today. Also, I got the cameras ready so that there will be a clear shoot of what the action is how things happen, as I have sex with the men. One of the things I do well is to make videos well, as it was the trade, I went into but since my husband makes more money than I will ever make, I never went after my dreams as in with a job. However, that does not mean I won't consider going into business with camera's and taking photos or videos of people.

Maybe that is what the plan is as in maybe my husband is trying to tell me a line of work I could do, however for this I am the subject, and I am the one who is getting the action. Although we will see, as I know of other women who have their own sex sites, but I don't know how much they make, but I assume it is enough to make them enough money to keep with what I would be saying that what may have started out as a hobby soon became their career of choice.

Waiting for someone to show up, I than got up and put another dollar bill to keep the videos going which in turn give me more time to be here. I than sat down as I did I than heard someone enter into the booth next to me, I than looked at the hole. I than got up and went to the hole to see if I could see anyone, and I did see a man on the other side, as he saw me, he then smiled as he did so.

I asked, "Do you want me to suck your cock for you?"

"Sure, that sounds good, here let me get my pants down for you and I also want to make sure the door is lock." He said, as he locked the door and pulled down his pants.

He then slides his cock though the hole, as he did so I than started to lick his cock as I took one of my hands as the other started to tape the whole thing. After I got the camera's rolling I than had his dick thrust as far back into my mouth as he could go, as I did so he started to do slight moans. Which made me smile I am quite good as giving head, but than anyone who loves sex can say the same.

As I used my tongue and mouth in a sucking action, as I slide back and forth on his cock, he started to grow larger and thicker than he was when we first started, I wanted him as large and thick as he is able to be. This way he will be able to fill my birth canal that I want so much for him to fill up, I am also sensing by the size of this man I want his child. Which is interesting as the idea was not to get pregnant, but I told my husband I won't be using any birth control or having them have a condom on, the idea would be to know full well that with every man that fucks me, he risks making me pregnant.

That risk was enough or is enough to make me hornier when my husband and I were talking. However, I want this man for some reason to make me be a mommy, not sure why. Maybe because his dick is large and more likely to make me pregnant, as the point to this is he will be deep inside me when he comes.

After a while once I got him to the point that he is as large and think as he could be I than took his cock out of my mouth, and I ask him, "Do you want to fuck me?"

"Fuck yes, but do you want me to use a condom or are you ok if I do you without one?" He asked, as I could tell he wanted to really fuck me.

I than answered him, "Yes please fuck me without one."

I than got up and I made sure that the camera still going, and everything was setup, I than took his cock, as I used it as a guide for me to use as I backup into the gloryhole. As I did so, I than could feel as his cock entered my very wet pussy, and as I slowly got him as deep inside of me as I could. I than started to use my body to do the thrusting as I slam my ass into the wall where the gloryhole is at with each thrust into me, he stays still as I did this.

With each thrust into me, I moan and panted as I want him deeper inside of me, as I tried to have him fuck me hard and deep, with what I have with me. He is as thick and as large as I can get him other than doing him on a bed or some sort of place where I can lay down on or me on top of him, I can only get him as far into me as I could with what I have here.

I rub my stomach as I felt where his cock was inside of me, with each thrust, as I did all the work for now, then I started to get a bit tired as I than stayed where I was, and he knew what needed to do next. As he started to fuck me, I moaned as I raise my head and my eyes rolled back with each thrust, he did to me, soon he started to really fuck me, making me louder both with my moans and with my pants.

As he did so, he started to moan as well, as well as grunt. As he did so I started to realizes that he is about to come inside of me, which than I started to get even more turned on as such I started to moan louder as I am about to take my first load inside of my pussy, that is if I decide that this will be it. However, I am enjoying this too much for me to say this will be my last load of the day.

As he pounds my pussy as if there is no tomorrow, I than started to have an orgasm, as I shout out, "Oh God you are about to make me come!"

"Then come with me babe as I am about to come as well." He said, as he did so my heart and mind started to get more and more high off of the sex that I am doing.

This would be my first man that I am with besides my husband, I don't feel as if I am cheating on him as he did indeed ask me to do this. I have to admit I am liking this, and perhaps being or becoming a slut is what I should have done before, well many years before. Not that I don't love my husband, I do but this is what he wanted me to become, however I can see why he wanted me to become this. Not for him but for myself, however I am starting to feel guilty as he is not here to watch as I am being fucked by another man.

But it is too late now, as I can feel as he is coming deep inside of me, as he does, we are both moaning and panting, with him grunting as well. As he comes I do as well, however even though he came inside of me, he is still very much thrusting in and out of me like before. Almost as if he wants to make sure every drop of his seed is inside of me.

He stayed inside me for a little while longer as he finishes coming inside of me, even till he was done, as he was done, he slowly took his cock out of me. Then he fingered fuck me a bit, and as he said so, he then asked me, "Do you come here regularly or is this your first time here?"

"This is my first time here why?" I asked, wondering if there is something more that can be done here.

He then answered me by saying this, "Well if you want my cock again, come in the mornings and I can for sure bring a couple more cocks for you to be banged by, think of it as a gang bang but with a glory hole."

I laughed and I said, "Sounds good, I will be here than, so in the morning time?"

"Yes around 11 am to about 5 pm depending on what is going on." He said, as he then raised up his pants and he then added, "Too be honest besides me, right now you're looking at gay men who want ass, but if that is what you want go ahead, I am sure they will not want to fuck you as they want a man to fuck his ass."

I than said, "Ok thank you for that advice and I guess we will see you tomorrow and maybe some of your friends as well?"

"Yes, we will and if you think my cock is large wait till you are being fucked by some of my friends." He said as I could tell he is getting ready to leave, he then added, "Do you want them to also fuck you without a condom as well, as we love girls who love it bareback?"

I than said, "Yes I want no condoms."

He laughed as he asked, "So the thrill of the unknown or of the risk that you could get pregnant is what is exciting you babe?"

"Yes, it is, besides I want to be surprise, and don't worry if I do get pregnant if that happens I won't seek you out." I said, as so he won't be afraid.

He laughed again, as he answered me, "Don't worry I help other women have the babies they wanted to have both as in a risk or just that they wanted to have a child with someone other than their spouse."

I than heard as he left the room, as he did so I than started to get everything packed up and ready to go, I than got dress and I have to plan the next day. After I had everything, I brought with me, and more I left both the booth and the store where I was and headed home. I than reported to my husband who is thrilled to know of what had happen and told me to go back tomorrow and to let them get me pregnant, as he wants me to be pregnant by someone else other than himself. I question this but if he wants me to be a slut than I guess this is part of the path.

After dinner my husband wanted me to go to bed naked and as I went to bed he came into the room, and he had some ropes with him, and he then said, "My love, Aedre tonight you will sleep naked, and tied to this bed, and during the night you will be done by men that I wish for you to be done by to prepare you for tomorrow."

"How many men are you going to have me be done by during the night?" I asked as he tied me to the bed.

He then smiled as he then answered me, "You will be done by two men tonight my dear, so that the total men that have done you will be three and depending on how many do you tomorrow at the gloryhole will determine how many do you tomorrow night as well."

As soon as I was tied up and ready for him to have the men that he wanted me to have sex with, at the doorway two naked men were there waiting for me, he then said to them as I could see what they look like, as both have huge members of their own, and he said, "Tonight please enjoy my wife sexual, and be free to fuck her anywhere you wish, as she is learning to be a slut and tonight is training for her big day tomorrow."

He then left the room and close the door, but there is enough light for them to fuck me, as both of them came closer I saw that they were already erected and ready to fuck the shit out of me, I thought to myself oh god they are going to make me pregnant. One of them went over in front of me, as he prepared himself to go inside of my pussy as the other moved my head over to his waiting cock as he gently slide his cock inside of my mouth, at the same time I felt the other men's cock glide into my pussy.

At the same time both men fucked me as one is in my mouth and the other in my pussy, they fucked me at the same time and speed, as they thrust into me at the same moment each time, they were slow at first but as I got used to them inside of me, they started to fuck me harder and faster, as they did so my heart race as they were huge inside of me, making the man earlier to be small.

After a bit, the one in my mouth stop but he has yet to come inside of me, and with the help of the one in my pussy they lifted me up as he slide under me, I than felt as his huge cocked enter my ass, as the one on top of me, than went down on me as the two of us kisses the other is now busy fucking my ass, as he does my ass he is necking me.

This happen the entire night as they fucked me this way, as I moan and scream in pleasure, my body is being prepared for more than just what I told my husband what will be happening tomorrow, I am being prepared for what I can say is perhaps a gang bang one that I myself will be the main course. Why I said is, is this why prepare my ass for having a guy in me, why tie me up, so the only reason is that my husband is preparing me for a gang bang at some point.

However, what happen the rest of the night is this, they came in me more than once, but only in my ass and pussy, at first it was hard to sleep but then with the orgasms and other things it became easy for me to sleep as with them thrusting in and out of me, the memories of my childhood as when my mother rocked me back and forth when I was sad or scared came back, as they did that to me now I soon fell asleep as they keep fucking me.

I woke up way before the time to get up, the two men were gone, and I was untied I was wearing what appeared to be some sort of diaper but other than that I was naked. I than went over and grab clean clothes for me to wear and I than went to the bathroom I took off my diaper and when I did it was filled up with cum inside of it, I smiled in a sick way I felt well used last night, but at the same time, I felt very much refresh and I have a lot of energy inside of me.

I showered and I than got myself ready for a new day, and a new adventure and one that I am sure that I will enjoy if not well, then this will be the last time I will try a glory hole, but then again, we will see. I do know this, that my body is now prepared to handle large cocks, than before, but I have no idea how many I will get today, or large they will be, as last night the two men that fucked me all night long were very large but then again, I don't have that much experience when it comes to sex anyways, other than what I have seen on porn or from friends of my.

However, one thing for sure, if this works out and with what I taped I feel that this is the choice I should do, why not make it where men fuck me as I tape it and then sell it on the Internet or on my own site. I smiled as I than sigh as I wish I had what happen to me tape that way I could have seen what they did to me as I slept. But anyways, I need to get ready, so as I did so I than started to get horny again, as I started to head out and back to the same book store that I had sex with the man yesterday.

Glory Hole Wife Aedre 2

Hello, again as some of you may know my name is Aedre and yesterday I did my first gloryhole season at a local adult bookstore which is where I am at now. I also had my first threesome with two men that my husband knows, whom he had me do. I am already in the same booth that I was in before, naked as well as ready for the next round of sex with more than one man.

As the first man I had sex with here, told me to come in the morning between a certain time frame I obeyed, and I am here ready as he said it will be more than him that will fuck me. So, I am now here waiting for him to show up, also he said that there would also be more than just him today as well. So, I wanted to make sure that he is good to his word.

In short, I will be having a gang bang of sorts but only one hole being used at a time, unless one of them comes in there with me as I am doing another, that would be the only other way for it to happen that way. However, anything and everything is possible when it comes to sex, heck we may even have sex somewhere else here.

Although this bookstore is no sex club, but they do have places that can support a gang bang or more here as well as other things. As I wait for whatever comes next, as I am already naked and I have place into the cash machine up front of the booth where the TV is at, I made sure that I have more than enough time to be here.

After waiting for what seemed like hours however I knew that it was just minutes as oppose to hours, the door to the booth next to me, where the hole is connected to opens up. I than got myself ready to jump up and then to come over to see who is on the other side and if it is who I am expecting to be there, or if it is another woman like me looking to be a slut and get cock inside of her.

However, as I looked onto the other side of the hole, I could see that it is a man, and he had a smile on his face as he unzipped his pants and pulled his pants and underwear down. I could tell that he knew I was watching and as he got himself ready, he then got himself towards the glory hole as I lick my lips as he put his cock into the hole.

I opened my mouth up, as he sided his cock deep down my throat as he did so I moved my mouth closer to the hole, that way he can do all the work. He then started to thrust on his own as he used my mouth as if it was a vagina which didn't bother me, as he did so he started to get himself larger and ready for what needed to be done.

As he started to slow down a bit, as I could tell he didn't want to come inside of my mouth and he said, "Man baby you know how to do this, however now I want to fuck your pussy."

I than took out his cock as I moved my mouth away from him and I than said, "Thank you for telling me I give good head, but now you will love my pussy as I am nice and wet as well as tight."

I didn't say any lie there as I am very tight and wet. As I got up and turned around, and as I did so I took one of my hands as the other I used to balance myself on the wall. As I took the other hand and wrap it around his cock, as I used both my hand and his head to guide myself to him. As his cock enter my waiting pussy I than slowly moved myself so that he was as deep as he could get than as my ass was up against the wall, he started to pound my pussy as the both of us moan.

With the sounds of everything else in the store, our moans which are quite loud as I am also crying out in passion as he uses my pussy to help himself. This guy is not the same man that did me yesterday, but I love his cock, and like yesterday I want to have his child. Not sure why but I rather have men who are fucking me that are not my husband to make me pregnant.

He then said, "Well babe your pussy is for sure tight I love it, I have to tell you that. However, when you are done let me in your booth as there are more coming who will be wanting to fuck you as well."

"Ok, but why do you want to be in here with me?" I asked, wondering.

He laughed as he said, "Let's just say I am glad I got to you first, anyways I want more of you and I can tell if your here you're looking for more than what you got or maybe something else."

I than said, "Yes your right well somewhat."

He then drilled deep into me which made me scream out in pleasure as I started to moan loud, he then said, "You need this I can tell, you have never been fucked this way before have you?"

"No, and there is a reason I am here." I answered as he slowed down a bit.

He keeps slowly fucking me as he asked, "Husband not giving any to you, or are you here to learn to be more of a slut, or what I can sense this isn't really your thing."

I sighed as I said, "Yes your right, my husband wants me to be more of a slut, but he barely fucks me."

"Hmm, let me tell you something ok." He said, as he said, "Once I finish inside of you get dress and I will get dress and come with me ok."

I than said, "Well my husband wants me to fuck a bunch of men here."

"Why?" He asked, as he said, "Why have you come here and making you have sex with other men, why doesn't he enjoy your body, why make you be fucked by other men, it's one thing if you want that but another if you are being told that he wants you to be a slut for him."

I than asked, "You want to take me to your place so you can fuck me, don't you?"

He laughed as he said this, "What gave you that idea, now by all means if you want other men to use you than stay but allow me to be in there with you, however if you wish to not do this here, but you still want to have other men have sex with you than I know a lot of men who would just love to have sex with you. Just by the way your pussy feels and by how you give oral. The thing is they will also treat you with respect and not treat you like an animal but as a human being."

I closed my eyes as how he is fucking me is more like how I was made love to the first time I had sex, however that was not with my husband. I than sighed as I than said, "Fine come inside of me and I will come with you."

He keeps doing me nice and slow and he said, "Babe what is your name?"

"Aedre." I answered as I gently moaned.

He then said, "Well Aedre once we are done let me take you to my place and talk about things a bit more."

"Ok." I said as he is now starting to thrust deeper and faster again.

After a bit he then moaned as I could tell he is about to come inside of me, as he went as far into me as he could as he stayed there as he filled me up. I started to orgasm as well, as his hot cum fills my womb, which has once more been feed again.

After we got done, we both got dress I didn't wipe myself as I wanted to keep the feeling of what we did still fresh on my mind. As I left the booth he did as well, and I have to say he is quite the hank way better than my husband is and much more someone I would rather be with. He smiled as I could see from his face and how he is making his facial features that he is also thinking the same thing as well.

He then said, "Well I wasn't really expecting you to look this hot, however I will say this whatever your husband wants from you to do all of this, I think for sure let's go to my place."

I than touch my pussy and asked, "You want to have sex with me again, don't you?"

"Well yes I do, but this time it will be at my place, and I can say this I can pleasure you a hell better than your husband will or could ever do." He said as he gave me his hand.

The two of us walked out of the bookstore as if we were a couple and it felt good in a sense, I am with a man that is acting more like my husband than my own husband does. He then leads me to his car which I can now see he is not poor at all but very rich he then opened the door for me to come in and I entered the back seat and he then opened up the front door and got inside.

I than asked him, "You drive yourself?"

"Yes, I like to do everything by myself, well I do have maids but well they don't know my life style." He said, and he then added, "I am not married at least yet, so they may assume you and I are courting however what I do with whomever is my business and they know well enough to not say anything."

I than asked, "So I am not the first that you are bring over to your place?"

He sighed as he answered me, "Depends on your point of view Aedre, yes you are not the first woman I have taken here to have sex with, however I am not just taken you to my place just for sex, I can sense what you need and as such I want to help you out."

I sighed as he started to take me to his place, I than said, "What do you sense about me, I mean my husband or my so called husband wants to change me into a slut."

"Is that who you are?" He asked me,

I than smiled and said, "No. However if I am not a slut why take me to your place to have sex with me?"

"Because you have just had sex not being made love to." He answered me.

I sighed again and I said, "But I am married you are asking for me to come live with you."

"Yes so your married, but to a man who wants you to fuck other men, so that you can be his slut!" he said, in a stern tone, he then said, "Aedre there is more than that he wants you away so he can fuck someone else, also look I will give you what you want, if you want to be a slut I will be there for you, I myself would be there as you enjoy men that I know that will make you feel not a slut but a goddess."

I than said, "You don't know who my husband is."

"I do." He answered me, as he said his name.

I gasp as I asked, "How do you know him and me?"

"Well, he made his money from someone let's just leave it like this, I made him rich, and I am much richer than he will ever be." He answered me.

I than asked, "Were you the man I did yesterday than, as he seemed different."

He sighed and said, "No I wish I was, as you won't have been in this mess, but I saved you from a mistake you would regret. I know about the threesome at your house and how he had you tied as men did you that you couldn't see, those men work for me and know my likes and told me about this. As your husband works for me, as well but not in the sex business I than looked more into this and found out about this morning and came as soon as I could."

"He wanted me to be gang bang there." I said to him,

He then said, "I know, but Aedre let me ask this, if you were my wife, I won't need to go there to find a one nigher or a couple of months' worth of a girl girlfriend. Become my wife Aedre, I can make it quick and sweet and without much fanfare, and if you want to be a slut for me, and it will be your choice than we can do it together, but I sense in you, that you want a man that can give you a child."

"Yes, I do." I said in a soft tone.

He stared at me as he looked at the mirror, he then said, "I thought so, I can tell you want a child from me and not your husband."

"I do." I said, as he seemed to already know this.

He then asked, "Tell me what you like as in terms of sexual stuff, I can tell glory holes isn't really your thing."

"Well like you said glory holes isn't my thing however, I guess I liked it last night as I was tied up as the two men fuck me." I answered him,

He then asked, "Do you think you are pregnant from what has happened not counting what we did today?"

"Other than the sex I did with you today, I don't think they made me orgasm other than last night but there were two of them, and not one." I said as I keep going for a bit, "I don't believe I am pregnant, as I just feel that it will take more than what happen last night or yesterday."

He then said, "Hmm, well from what you are telling me you don't feel your pregnant from what has happen, since you and I meet."

"Yes." I said,

He then keeps driving as we did, we got to this gate where he entered a code as he did the gate opened up and I than saw his house, God he has to be rich to live here. As we got to the driveway of his mansion, that is when I realizes I married the wrong man, as I am now with my husband's boss and not only that he has fucked me once already.

He then stopped the car and he then asked me, "Aedre have you ever been fucked in a car before?"

"No." I responded back to him.

He then grins as he asked me, "Do you want too?"

I giggled as I said, "Sure why not."

"Then take off your clothes and lay on the seat and don't worry about if you get cum on the cushion." He said, as he opened his door.

I than undid my seat belt as I than took off the clothes I had one and place them on the door nearest me which I will used as a pillow. Naked and laying on my back as I moved my legs into a position where he or anyone else for that matter could easily have access to my vagina. He got out and then went over to the other door and opened it up.

He then took off his clothes right there and then for all to see him get naked, and he place his clothes on the floor of the car where he is nearest too, than he went inside the car, as he climbed in and came onto of me he then places his cock inside of me once more as him and I started to kiss, as we kisses I put my arms around him as we had sex.

I won't call this fucking we were making love, as this was way more passionate than just what I have done in the last two days. As we kiss as he slowly thrust in and out of me, I have never made love like this before, as for the first time, I wanted him to be mine. As we stopped kissing for a while, and I smiled as we both looked at each other he then started to neck me as he sucked on my neck as he started to speed up making me start to crawl into his back.

I let out, "Oh God I am about to cum fuck me, fuck me harder I want you to make me pregnant. I want you as my husband!"

After that he keep doing what he was doing, with my neck as he started to go down harder as he fucked me harder, as he did, I went wild as I could help myself, as I started to come as he also was drawing closer to coming inside of me as well. Then he started to grunt and moan as he then came in me. I lost myself for a bit as the feeling was great and I just wanted him in me, as he was still slowly thrusting in me giving me pleasure as my mind and body started to relax.

It was a bit later when he got off of me as he then got out of the car and still naked as he went over to the side of the car where I had my head against I than had the strength to move over he opened the door and I got out naked like he is, as my bare feet meet the concert I kind was uncomfortable, however he seemed fine with it.

I than asked, "Should we at least get shoes or something on, and what about others seeing us naked like this?"

He smirks as he said, "Like I said my maids and staff won't care if your naked, why don't you follow me keep your things in there I will have one of my servants get your things for you."

I nodded as I followed him into the house, and the odd part is I didn't care if I was naked, and him saying that gave me a new found strength that I didn't believe I had in me, as I followed him into the mansion he opened the door as if he has done this many times while naked. Looking into the mansion it is quite nice and well suited for children that I could have with him.

As the two of us went inside of the huge building, some of his servants came over to him, they acted as if they see this many times before, and they smiled when they saw me. One of them said in a kind tone, "I see you brought home to us a beautiful one, do you wish for us to prepare her a room?"

"Yes, please but I want her in the master room, with everything." He said,

I wondered what he meant by everything, as they all went their ways to get things prepared, he then took my hand and brought me upstairs there he went into a room. As he opened it up, the room appeared quite well keep, however it also appears to not be used much. He then went over to the bed and sat down, I than entered the room and closed the door.

He then asked, "Did you like being tied up as you had a threesome?"

"I did." I answered,

He then smiled, as he asked another question, "Would you like more than me to have sex with you or just me?"

I than grin as I said, "Well I know I said I didn't wish to become a slut but yes I liked being fucked by other men at the same time, I am not sure if I want to do a glory hole again or not, but you have opened my eyes to see a much wider view of what can be done with sex."

"Aedre, you given me an idea of what you want but unlike your husband or so called husband, I want to please you I want you happy and not to feel as if you have to become a slut in order to please me." He said,

I smiled as I said, "You opened my eyes, and I see that yes I know you want me happy, what my husband wanted I can see and sense that now, he wanted me not there he wanted me to be a slut and as such he could leave me. As for you, I want to become your slut, and I liked being tied up and I liked having men fuck me, but I want you to watch me as well as to fuck me as they too fuck me."

He nodded as he then said, "I understand now, lay down and I will get you ready."

I than obeyed as I laid down, he then took out from under the bed restraints as he used them to tie me up as he had me in a position where a guy could have a choice either my pussy or my ass. As well as the fact that one could be fucking my mouth, as he made sure I am comfortable, he then moved back away from the bed.

I expected him at least to come over to me as I am helpless and can't go anywhere, I thought he would take my pussy once more, but he just smirks as to see what I would do or say. Then three men came into the room with us, and they like the two of us are naked, their cocks already erected and ready to fuck me.

I gasp at the size of their cocks, as my body twitch and I grasp onto the bonds that hold me, as they were surely make me come, as well as to get me pregnant. I didn't want anyone else getting me pregnant now, other than him the one whose mansion I am in. I didn't understand why he wanted me to have sex with them, before I am pregnant with his child. I don't care where I have sex after I am pregnant with his child, hell I would even go back to the glory hole and have them all fuck me.

He then asked, "Aedre can you let them take your mouth and ass?"

I smiled as I answered him, "Yes, but I want you to make me pregnant."

"I will be, as they will only be doing your mouth and ass." He told me,

After that he went over to the wall naked as he nodded, as he did so the three men, who are already very erected came over to me, and one of them went up in front where he has access to my ass and pussy, he then started to lube me up as the other two went on either side of me, as they started to touch my breast and as one sided his cock inside my waiting mouth.

I closed my eyes as I waited for the large cock to enter my ass, as I felt the head start to enter my anus and traveled with ease into my bowls as he did, so I grasp to the ropes that held me in place. Unable to moan or cry out in pleasure all I did was mumbled moans as my mouth is being used as a pussy as he is fucking my mouth.

I have become what a gay bottom is, but I have a pussy and can have kids. As the man in my ass, started to fuck me harder I could sense is he nearing to start to fill my bowels with his seed. As I mumbled moans and pants as I closed my eyes as I am being rocked back and forth as I held onto the ropes with both hands.

As my mouth is being used, I could now feel as the man in my ass started to come deep inside me, as he is thrusting inside of me, as he did so he didn't stop fucking my ass, either he loves my ass too much or something else. Then he stopped as he did one massive thrust taking his cock as deep inside of me as he could as he finishes coming inside of me.

Once he was done, the one in my mouth came out of me, and the other man went into my mouth, as the taste of cock was for sure in my mouth, as the one in my ass went out of me, and the one in my mouth than started to fuck me. With both the lube in my ass, and the cum from the first man, as the next guy just slide inside of my ass without any issue.

He went as deep as the first as he started to fuck me nice and slow, then he started to pound my ass as he did, he made me rock back and forth much more than the first guy. Which made the one in my mouth having to take his cock out of my mouth, so I don't accidental bite him, as I swing back and forth like I am.

As I swing back and forth with each thrust into me, I am moaning and crying out in pleasure, as I have my mouth wide open, and my eyes shut as I am being ass fucked. Then like the man before him he started to add to the amount of cum inside of my bowels, as he came, I could feel and taste his cum as the smell came up from my bowels to my stomach.

Unload his seed into her already filled stomach, he stayed in her as she once more had another cock in her mouth as she stays still as he uses her mouth as he did, as the one in her ass stays there for a bit longer. As he wishes to make sure every drop of his seed is inside my bowels, he than exited her as his seed stays deep inside of her.

Once he leaves her ass and moves away with the first man, as she opens her eyes to see that the other two are just waiting for the last man left to do his thing, as he sided his cock out of me and went over to my ass, she could tell he is about to come, and wanted to come in my mouth but knew that he is to empty in my ass and not my mouth.

He then did one or two thrust into her as he started to come, filling me again. As he then went out of my ass and then went over to the other three men as the three of them left me hanging above the bed, than my lover comes over looking me over as I had three men use my ass and mouth he then smiled as he could see that I have been used well. As my body just needs a cock inside of my pussy and then I will orgasm, releasing an egg and making me a mother.

He came over to me slapping his rock hard cock on my stomach as he teased me, than he entered my pussy pushing it deep inside of me making me moan and yelling out, "Oh God yes fuck me, please I want your child please fuck me!"

He then started to thrust nice and slow as he went down as the two of us started to kiss once more and once both of us were comfortable, he started to fuck me hard, as he did so my muffed moans were still heard in the room as he is making me pregnant now. I than started to orgasm as my body couldn't handle it anymore, his cock going deep inside of me, like it has done so more than once already.

Nothing I could say or do now, won't change anything I am now his, I am now going to be a mother all he now needs to do is come inside of me, which there is no stopping that now. My body now started to orgasm more and more even my ass joined in, I quaked and shook from head to toe, I have become his.

The last thing I recall before I pass out was him starting to come deep inside of my womb, which made sure that he made me pregnant that I am now going to be a mommy. That he is going to be a father, and I felt he will soon be my husband and I will be his wife. I than blacked out as another wave of orgasms rocked my body, and my body couldn't handle it no longer.

I than awake not sure how long I was out I was no longer tied up, I am still naked but I been washed and clean up. I smelled like oranges and a fruit like smell was all around me. I felt clean and I also felt well rested, I am laying down on another bed, which looks larger than the other. I slowly get up, I am still sore, but it is all good, I also feel the afterglow of the sex I just had.

Unlike the times before he has always made love to me and not fucked me like the men that has done me in the past. Once I got up and looked around in the room, I saw him sitting down not far away from the bed. He is smiling as he stood up, he like myself am still naked. He has in one hand a small box which looks like it could have a ring in it.

He then came over to me and kneel down as he handed it to me, I opened it and it was a ring that is made very well and has a diamond, this is a ring that my husband couldn't afford. He then said, "I want to be your husband, if you are wondering about your ex-husband, it's all taken care of. Please marry me, Aedre and whatever you want sexual or anything I will give you."

I smiled as I looked at him and I said, "Yes I will be your wife, I want many babies from you. However please forgive me, but I have become what my ex-husband wanted me to become."

"Its fine, and while it happens, I will be with you." He said, almost as if he knew that would be the case.

I than asked, "Are you sure, I mean you would be sharing me with other men?"

"Aedre, I make love to you, the others only fuck you, and as such it is fine, and I want to share you." He said,

I nodded as I said, "I understand."

He got up and the two of us hugged as the two of us started on a new journey together, soon we will be husband and wife, as well as mother and father. I could sense that he made me pregnant, and I love every moment of this, as I know that our child will have a loving family for him or her to be raised in. My life has for sure gotten better as now I feel I am with a husband or soon to be a husband that cares for me, unlike before who wanted me to become what he wanted me to become and not what was for the good.

The End

www.ingramcontent.com/pod-product-compliance
Lightning Source LLC
Chambersburg PA
CBHW081150160726
47997CB00021B/3157